BIONICLE®

Inferno

by Greg Farshtey

SCHOLASTIC INC.
New York Toronto London Auckland Sydney
Mexico City New Delhi Hong Kong Buenos Aires

For Debbie and Roy

ISBN: 0-439-82805-8

12 11 10 9 8 7 6 5 4 3 2   7 8 9/0

Printed in the U.S.A.
First printing, December 2006

Introduction

100,000+ Years Ago

Two cloaked figures walked silently through a vast underground chamber. They had traveled far to reach this spot, starting from a place whose forges burned hotter than the stars themselves. They had traversed the domains of Artakha and Karzahni, crossed vast wastelands that would someday teem with life, until finally they reached their intended destination. All along the way they were watchful, for the path was dangerous and the cargo they carried priceless.

Their journey had brought them to the center of a large continent. All around them, the biomechanical beings they had named Matoran were hard at work at an assortment of tasks. They took no notice of the newcomers, for that is how the two travelers wished it.

"Is this wise?" one asked the other.

"Wise, and something even rarer than that," came the answer. "It is practical."

The smaller of the two figures raised his weapon and blasted a hole in the ground. Again, the Matoran took no notice. He fired again, creating the beginnings of a tunnel in the earth. As he did so, his partner stood to the side, holding the golden shell in which their treasure resided.

The work of blasting and tunneling went on for some hours, with hours more spent carving a great staircase that traveled the length of the tunnel. At the bottom of the stairs, the grim figure increased the power of his weapon and blasted a huge chamber into existence.

"Is this far enough down?" he asked.

The second figure nodded. "We want it to take them time to reach the bottom, but not all of their days."

Both figures shed their cloaks. The new chamber was ringed by canals of molten lava and the heat was stifling. The golden shell was placed on the ground, gently, as the two set to work building a pedestal for it out of a piece of stone. When they were done, the taller figure opened the shell slowly and hesitantly as if its contents might explode.

"Be careful!" said the other. "You remember what happened the last time someone touched it."

"I do indeed. It was a useful lesson in the need to respect objects of power. Now keep quiet a moment, or we will get a second lesson courtesy of our creation."

Unlimbering special tools, the figure pried apart the shell to reveal a Kanohi mask inside. On the surface, it seemed not so very much different from dozens of other Masks of Power. But where other masks might be useful tools or powerful weapons, this one had the power to give life to a universe . . . or to obliterate it.

Steeling himself for what was to come next, he grasped the mask with the ends of the two tools. Energy flowed up the shafts and into the figure, sending intense pain through his form. But he did not scream. He would not, he decided, give something he had made the satisfaction of knowing it had hurt him.

Ignoring the agony, he used the tools to lift the mask into the air and deposit it on the pedestal. Then he quickly withdrew his hold of the object. The mask rested in its appointed place now, where it was destined to remain until needed.

"It's not enough," said the smaller figure. "We can bury it deep, even provide Umbra as a protector for it. But can we be sure it is safe here?"

"We will do what we must," his partner replied. "Mata Nui will one day face challenges we cannot even imagine, in places we can only dream of. If one of those challenges proves to be too great even for his power, this Mask of Life may be all that can save him."

"All the more reason to guard —"

"The mask will make its own guardians, as it needs them. You know that. Be assured, the

Mask of Life will never leave this chamber until the destined time."

"Then it's time for us to leave," said the smaller figure, putting his weapon away. "I prefer not to be so close to it."

"Afraid of something you made yourself?"

"I've seen what the mask can do . . . how far it will go to protect itself. I am still not convinced that we can prevent anyone from taking it before its time — but I pity anyone who tries."

With a final look at the Mask of Life, the two figures departed the chamber and started the long climb back to the surface. This would be their last visit to the continent, and though their passage went unnoticed, they and their kind were not unknown. In centuries to come, Matoran would speak in wonder of the Great Beings who brought Mata Nui into existence and charged him to watch over the universe.

And the Mask of Life? It would be taken from its chamber only once in 100 millennia. When it was seen what the mask could do, it

was swiftly returned with a mixture of gratitude and horror. There it remained, until one
demented, doomed being dared to attempt its
theft — and paid for it. Now mask and mad being
lurk down below, waiting for the day someone
else will attempt to summon the energies of the
Mask of Life.

Waiting until now . . .

ONE

The crimson-armored Piraka named Hakann was trying hard to think. When in a dangerous situation, he knew, it was important to clearly and logically consider events and plan your next steps. And it would have been much easier to do if someone weren't screaming.

It took a few moments for Hakann to realize the screams were coming from his own mouth.

Stop it! Hakann yelled at himself. *Stop behaving like some pathetic Matoran, and act like the murderous, treacherous Piraka that you are!*

What had happened? How had he gone from being in control to being a total, horror-stricken wreck, sitting on a staircase with his armor melting off him?

He made a mental leap to grab a shred of reality still floating around in his brain. Yes, now he remembered. The six Piraka had discovered the hidden entrance to a huge stone stairway. The stairs, they had been told, led down to a Chamber of Life where the powerful Kanohi Ignika was hidden. The Ignika, or Mask of Life, was the prize they had come to Voya Nui to find and steal.

There were complications, of course. After demolishing a team of Toa Nuva, the Piraka had encountered a second team of Toa on the island. These Toa Inika wielded lightning along with their other powers and actually proved to be a challenge. But the Piraka had still managed to get a head start down the staircase.

Hakann was in the lead. He knew it was potentially fatal to turn his back on his partners. But the one who made it to the chamber first would get his claws on the mask first. He decided that was worth the risk.

He had made his way down a few dozen stairs, navigating by the glow of lightstones embedded in the walls, when he came to a fork in the staircase. The left passage was blocked with stone, but the right was open, so he went right. Suddenly, something flew at him from out of the darkness, too fast for him to dodge. As it struck him, he realized it looked like a zamor sphere. Had one of the other Piraka somehow gotten ahead of him to stage an ambush?

No, that wasn't it, he realized. Zamor spheres didn't make you feel like this. Hakann felt like the world was rushing by him and he was standing still. He felt dizzy and sick and warm . . . then searingly hot . . . as if the flame power he commanded had been unleashed inside him. He staggered backward, already seeing his armor starting to soften and run like rock in a lava pool. The pain was agonizing. Some little voice in his head was saying that this made no sense, because his organic tissue wasn't near enough to his armor to be affected. The rest of him was too busy yelling in shock and pain.

Now something was lumbering up the stairs toward him. It was impossibly big and broad and the light glinted off its golden head and spine.

Golden spine? . . . That would mean . . . no, that's just a myth!

But it was no fable approaching, teeth bared in a savage smile, claws ready to rip and tear. It was the nightmare of every member of Hakann's species — a legendary denizen of the darkness who lived to destroy. It was a creature of myth that had never existed . . . but it lived here and now, and Hakann couldn't help but scream its name.

"Irnakk!"

The Piraka turned and fled then, melted armor dripping on the stairs as he ran. He stumbled before he reached the top of the stairs. He could hear Irnakk coming up behind him. Desperate, Hakann tried to huddle in a corner. *Maybe it won't see me,* he reasoned, as he shut his eyes tight. *Maybe . . . maybe it will be content just to kill the others.*

And the sound of footsteps came closer, and closer, and closer. . . .

"What happened to him?" asked Thok, looking down at the terrified Hakann. "Is this some trick?"

"Hakann!" Zaktan snapped. "Stop screaming and tell us what happened!"

Reidak tapped Zaktan on the shoulder and pointed down the stairs. "I think that happened."

The monstrous being called Irnakk appeared. Its laugh tore at the Piraka's sanity.

"No . . ." breathed Avak.

"Impossible," said Zaktan.

Irnakk bellowed. The sound stabbed at the Pirakas' minds like a sword of fire. If they didn't believe in it before, they had to accept the reality of this monster now.

"How can this be?" asked Thok, preparing for combat even as raw fear clutched at his heart. "Everyone knows there's no such thing as Irnakk!"

"Tell it that," snarled Avak. "Maybe you can get it to agree it doesn't exist."

The brown-armored Piraka reached out with his power to create a prison around the advancing Irnakk. Before it could take shape, one of the multiple zamor spheres mounted on Irnakk's shoulders took flight. It struck Avak dead center. Just that quickly, Avak found he could not move or speak. He was trapped, and his own body was his prison cell.

"No such thing, says you?" Irnakk growled in a voice like bones cracking. "As real as pain and death, says I."

Thok thought fast. What happened in the myths? How was Irnakk defeated? Then he realized that all the tales told by his species ended the same way — Irnakk slaughters everyone in sight and leaves only when there is no one left to demolish.

All right, if I can't stop him, I'll slow him down, the white-armored Piraka decided. He used his power on the tunnel walls, aiming to bring them to life and crush Irnakk between them.

Another zamor sphere fired from Irnakk's body. When it struck, Thok could feel his power being blocked and reversed. The next moment, his own armor came to life and began to squeeze. He felt the breath being forced out of his lungs. Thok gasped, but couldn't get any air. He was being crushed by his own power and couldn't stop it.

"Back to the surface!" Zaktan yelled. "Let it have these three!"

Reidak and Vezok were already on the run, deserting their leader and their partners. Two more zamor spheres caught them in the back. Instantly, they turned and started battling each other. Vezok pummeled Reidak with a rock until the black-armored Piraka went down. But Reidak's power to adapt would not let him stay defeated for long. He was back on his feet, slamming Vezok into the walls repeatedly until his enemy fell. Reidak smiled.

Then the smile disappeared. Battered and twisted, Vezok rose again. He had absorbed Reidak's power to adapt after defeats and to fight anew. Reidak charged back into battle, already knowing this fight could never end.

Zaktan stopped in mid-flight. He could transform himself into a swarm of protodites and slip past the battling Vezok and Reidak, but now he knew there was no point. There would be no escape from Irnakk . . . not this way.

The leader of the Piraka turned to face the

only thing he feared. Irnakk towered over him, eyes gleaming with satisfaction. "What are you?" asked Zaktan. "How did you escape from the world of legend to this desolate place?"

Irnakk's answer was a burst of crimson light from his eyes that enveloped Zaktan. The power cascaded over the Piraka's form, transforming him from physical matter to a being of pure thought. He no longer had any substance, but was just a fleeting wisp, like a half-remembered idea. An instant later, he felt a sensation of movement and he was suddenly somewhere else.

Picture the most complicated maze in existence, where slimy walls throbbed with life. Imagine a place that thundered with the sounds of madness, so loud the noise threatened to shatter the skull. Try to conceive of a place where the "air" was so heavy and thick that taking a step felt like walking underwater. Add all of this together and an image might form that was one-tenth of what Zaktan experienced in his new home.

I'm in Irnakk's mind, the Piraka realized with

horror. *It turned me into a thought and . . . drew me into its mind.*

An explosion rocked the walls, sending Zaktan flying. He felt like his head would burst from the sound. His lungs burned. At first, he thought perhaps someone had attacked Irnakk. Then the truth came to him — the convulsion in Irnakk's mind had not been the result of an impact. That had been Irnakk conceiving an idea.

"Welcome, Zaktan." Irnakk's voice boomed throughout the caverns and tunnels of its brain. "Be grateful you are . . . on my mind, for now. If I should decide to think of something else . . . you won't even exist as a thought."

"What do you want?" Zaktan whispered — or screamed. He could no longer tell the difference. "What are you?"

A second explosion, more violent than the first, battered the Piraka. That was not an idea being born, that was a memory. Zaktan could feel new knowledge flooding his being. This portion of the stairway leading to the Mask of Life fed off of a traveler's fears. Whatever filled them with the most horror would come to life, and true life, not mere illusion. For the Piraka, that was Irnakk.

The answer seemed easy. Stop being afraid of Irnakk and it would disappear. *And I will do that,* Zaktan thought, *right after I stop breathing.*

The six Toa Inika advanced cautiously down the first few steps, keeping an eye out for ambushes. They were sure the Piraka had beaten them here and might be lying in wait anywhere along the way.

"We have to quick-move," said Kongu. "If they beat us to the mask —"

"Vakama led the Toa Metru into a trap," Jaller replied. "Tahu Nuva charged ahead and got himself poisoned. I won't continue that particular Toa of Fire tradition."

"You don't have to," said Matoro. "I'll be back in a moment."

"Matoro! Wait!" Jaller yelled. But it was too late. The Toa of Ice's body sagged and hit the ground. Matoro had once more used his mask power to unleash his spirit. "Makuta bones, what's the matter with him?" Jaller grumbled. "What if there's something down there he can't just fly through?"

"You'll have to trust he knows what he's doing," said Hahli.

"I know I am trying to be more open to my teammates' ideas than maybe Tahu and Vakama were in the past," Jaller shot back. "But the team has to have a leader. Toa can't just go off on their own in the middle of a dangerous situation —"

"I'll keep that in mind," said Matoro, sitting up. "In the meantime, you might be interested to know that there's a huge monster down below who seems to have beaten five Piraka. Zaktan's nowhere to be seen."

"One monster, instead of six Piraka?" said Hewkii. "Sounds like the odds have improved."

"Hope someone tells the beast-monster that," muttered Kongu.

Zaktan felt himself being hurled forward at high speed. The next thing he knew, he was standing in front of Irnakk again, once more a physical being.

"You taste stale," said Irnakk. "I spat you out."

"Now what?" asked Zaktan, struggling to regain his bearings. "Do you kill us?"

Irnakk laughed. "Where is the fun in that, says I? Alive, you can fill the air with the music of your screams. Dead, you are just silent meat."

Zaktan nodded. "You exist because of our fear, don't you? And if we stop fearing you, you stop living."

"True," Irnakk replied. "But you can never free yourself from your fear of me."

"There is one thing that can free us all," Zaktan said, looking up at the ceiling. "One blast of my eyebeams in the right place, and this whole ceiling comes crashing down. I and my partners die . . . and with us, our fear . . . and with our fear, you."

Irnakk laughed. "A fine game you play. But if your horror of me does not stop you, your horror of death will. I have haunted the night-mares of your kind long enough to know that."

Zaktan's expression darkened with rage. "You think you know horror, Irnakk? Horror is looking into the eyes of the Shadowed One, knowing you are about to die . . . and then being forced to live. Horror is waking each day to see every part of your body moving on its own, a shifting mass of protodites where once was solid metal and living tissue. Horror is what is in the eyes of your partners when they look at you . . . and in the cries of your enemies when your swarm engulfs them. Don't talk to me about fear, creature — I *am* fear!"

Irnakk hurled a zamor sphere at Zaktan, then another. The Piraka's body formed open-ings to allow the spheres to fly straight through without doing any harm.

"No, no," said Zaktan, moving closer to his enemy, eyes sizzling with power. "This nightmare is over now, one way or the other. Let us pass, Irnakk, or die."

Even as he said the words, Zaktan knew Irnakk could stop him before he carried out his threat. But strangely, the monster was not acting. Instead, it almost looked satisfied.

"You use fear as a weapon, the same as I," Irnakk said. "I make you fear life, and in return, you make me fear death. You have found your true being — your essence is darkness and the grave, Piraka. The pit yawns for you, and who am I to keep you and yours from it?"

Zaktan sensed the other five Piraka standing behind him, whole and as sane as they ever had been. *The Mask of Life is testing us,* he thought. *This was only the first challenge, and it almost destroyed us.*

Irnakk began to fade from view. Zaktan took no comfort in the victory, knowing the Piraka were still a long way from their goal.

On the other hand, he said to himself, *the Toa will never even make it this far. The beings most likely to be destroyed by fear are those who won't admit to having any.*

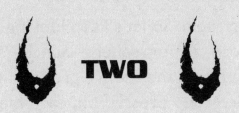

TWO

Garan led the other five members of the Matoran resistance through the winding corridors of the Piraka stronghold. They could still hear the sounds of battle coming from the virus chamber, though they were unsure who was fighting.

"We should go back," said Dalu. "This fight is for our freedom. We should be part of it."

"We are part of it," said Garan, "a very important part. The Toa Inika tasked us with finding the imprisoned Toa Nuva. If the Inika fall, the Nuva may be the only hope we have."

"But why look here? They could have the Nuva hidden anywhere on the island!"

Velika chuckled. "When you fear the Muaka, it is best to keep him in sight."

"He's right," said Balta. "The Piraka would want such dangerous foes where they could keep an eye on them. So let's keep looking. And don't drop those zamor sphere launchers — I built them in a hurry and they're pretty fragile."

The group pressed on, each member well aware that their quest might be futile. The Toa Inika weren't even sure that the Toa Nuva were still alive — just hopeful.

Then again, thought Garan, *in some battles, hope is the only weapon you have.*

The Toa Inika stood before a fork in the stairway. The right passage was blocked with stone, and the left wide open.

"Think the Piraka closed off the right passage to throw us off the trail?" asked Jaller.

Hewkii took a close look at the pile of rock. "No, this has been here a long time."

Matoro frowned. He could have sworn that when he came this way in his spirit form, the *left* passage had been blocked and the *right* open. Given what Hewkii said, though, that was impossible . . . wasn't it?

"So we go left," Jaller said.

"Great," muttered Kongu. "Guess I am the only one who remembers what Turaga Matau always says about going left."

Before the Toa could take a step into the left portal, Jaller spotted a figure coming up the staircase toward them. "Be ready!" he snapped, and the other Inika braced for combat.

But the being that emerged from the shadows was not a Piraka or some other kind of enemy. He was an almost regal figure in red and gold armor, wearing an all too familiar Kanohi Mask of Shielding. The shield he carried somehow managed to gleam brightly even in the dim light. Although none of the Toa Inika present had any memories of ever meeting him before, they all recognized him from the Turaga's tales.

"This is impossible," Jaller whispered. "Toa Lhikan??"

"Wait, wait a minute," said Matoro. "Turaga Vakama said Lhikan became a Turaga 1000 years ago, fought Makuta, and . . ."

"The word you're hard-looking for is 'died,'" said Kongu, taking aim with his laser crossbow. "Which means the golden one here is an impostor."

The figure before them made no move to defend himself. He regarded the Toa Inika calmly and when he spoke, it was with an almost paternal tone to his voice. "Amazing . . . that the Toa Metru I helped bring in to being should lead to a new generation of heroes with such . . . unusual masks."

"Who are you?" demanded Hahli. "You cannot be who you appear to be. Toa Lhikan died a hero, and you defile his memory."

"And his mask!" said Jaller. He had inherited the Noble Mask of Turaga Lhikan, but it was stolen from him during the journey to Voya Nui.

"Am I dead in your memories? Am I dead in your hearts?" asked Lhikan. "Because if the answer to those questions is no, then I am not truly dead."

"If I quick-fire this crossbow, you will be," replied Kongu.

Lhikan ignored him. "I've come to bring you a warning. Proceed no farther down these stairs. The Mask of Life is not for such as you. Turn back, Toa, while you can."

Jaller looked into the eyes of the Toa he regarded as one of the greatest heroes in history. All he saw was shadow. "If you truly are Toa Lhikan, would you turn back and give up on so vital a mission, when you know thousands depend on you?"

Lhikan shook his head. "No, I wouldn't," he said, taking a step backward into the darkness. "But, then, look what happened to me."

Jaller rushed forward, but Toa Lhikan was gone. The Toa Inika of Fire turned back to his comrades, troubled and confused. "First Karzahni, now this . . . far too many specters of the past trying to stop us."

"Well, we have to worry about the future . . . they don't," said Nuparu. "So let's keep going."

The Toa Inika continued down the staircase, convinced that they could now leave the past behind them. Unfortunately, they were about to discover the past was far from through with them.

* * *

Axonn had spent a lot of time lately on the wrong end, of battles. His first clash with the Piraka had ended, thanks to an ambush by Brutaka. His efforts to stop Brutaka from revealing the location of the Mask of Life had resulted in his being beaten to a pulp by a being he used to consider a friend.

But in this game, Brutaka, it doesn't matter who wins the first few battles, Axonn thought. *Only who wins the last one.*

Brutaka charged. Axonn swung his axe, only to have his enemy block it with a twin-bladed sword. Weapons locked together, they strained at each other. Brutaka had the advantages of height and reach, but Axonn was a little stronger and rapidly began to force his enemy back.

"You're weakening," said Axonn.

"You're dreaming," Brutaka shot back.

"Give up. There's no reason Botar has to be brought into this."

Brutaka's eyes widened. Every Order of Mata Nui member knew the name Botar, and just what mention of him could mean. "You wouldn't," he said.

"Watch me."

"I'd rather watch you die," said Brutaka, suddenly stopping his resistance. With nothing pushing back, Axonn's own force propelled him forward. Brutaka fell backward and used his legs and Axonn's momentum to send his enemy flying. Axonn hit the floor and skidded close to the crystal vat containing the Piraka's virus.

Brutaka got to his feet and raised his sword. It was time to finish the job.

Axonn saw the blade coming toward him. He rolled aside at the last possible moment as the tip of Brutaka's sword buried itself in the floor. Axonn used a leg sweep to upend Brutaka. As soon as his foe hit the ground, Axonn tried to wrest the sword away.

"Stupid," said Brutaka. "You gave this sword to me, remember? Already forgotten what it can do?"

The weapon flared with energy. An electrical jolt shot through Axonn's body, forcing his hands to tighten on the sword. Pain ripped through him and he couldn't let go!

"I could just let you fry," Brutaka snarled, even as he kicked Axonn's axe across the room. "When did you become such a fool? I've beaten you twice. . . . This will be the last time."

Brutaka shut down the blade's energy. Axonn gasped and let go of the weapon.

"When the Piraka return with the Mask of Life, I'm taking it away from them," Brutaka said. "Then I am getting off this barren rock and showing the universe what real power looks like. And you're not going to do anything to stop me."

Brutaka called on the power of his Kanohi mask. A dimensional vortex appeared in the air near Axonn, moving closer and closer to the downed guardian.

"Why should I waste my blade on you, when I can transport you far from here?" Brutaka asked, laughing. "Go ahead, Axonn, attack me. Even if you knock me out, that gate will keep after you until it draws you inside. It won't disappear until someone has passed through it . . . and that someone is you."

Axonn saw the gate advancing rapidly, threatening to envelop him. He couldn't see anything inside it, only deep darkness. He knew Brutaka's power — the gate might lead to someplace else on Voya Nui or any other island, or even to a different dimension entirely. No matter the destination, he knew he would wind up too far away to stop Brutaka.

Axonn scrambled to his feet and prepared for a final charge at his enemy. *All right, Brutaka — but if I have to go, you can bet I'm not going alone.*

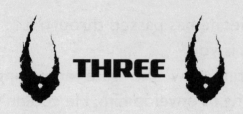

THREE

Toa Matoro barely ducked in time. A blast of shadow energy tore through the rock above his head. The near miss wasn't half as disturbing as who hurled the blast.

"Okay, this can really stop!" he shouted. "Any time now would be fine!"

The Toa Inika had rounded a bend in the staircase only to find themselves face-to-face with a host of nightmares. Blocking their way were a Rahkshi, a Bohrok, a Bohrok-Kal, a Nui-Rama, a Muaka, and at the head of this assemblage of evil, Makuta himself. All were beings they had faced before as Matoran, but their presence here as a team made no sense. There was little time to puzzle it out, though, as a hail of shadow bolts, fire blasts, fear power, and more drove the Toa Inika back.

"Lhikan wasn't joking," said Kongu. "And

30

here I always thought reunions were supposed to be happy-fun."

Toa Hahli narrowly dodged the slashing claws of the Muaka, a great catlike animal. She responded to the attack with one of her own, a powerful blast of water that slammed into the Rahi beast and hurled him against the rock wall. The Muaka struck hard and slid to the ground, unmoving.

Hahli's eyes widened. The creature looked dead, but she had seen Muaka get hit by much worse and spring right back into action. The awful thought that she did not know her own strength as a Toa ran through her head.

"Hey, Hahli!" yelled Hewkii. "This is no time to daydream!"

"You take the Bohrok," Kongu said to Hewkii. "I want the big guy for myself."

Farther up the stairs, Jaller was wrestling with a Rahkshi Turahk. The red-armored creature with its power to induce fear was a challenge, but still an enemy that a prepared Toa could handle with some effort. Yet Jaller felt his muscles turning to water as he fought the monster. Memories of another fight with a Turahk kept intruding.

He had been a Matoran then, side by side with the Toa Nuva and his best friend, Takua, on the island of Mata Nui. Makuta had sent his Rahkshi to try to stop the Toa of Light from ever coming into being. A Turahk had been about to strike down Takua when Jaller grabbed on to the Rahkshi's staff. Pure fear power poured into Jaller until it overwhelmed his ability to handle it. He died then, only to be returned to life later in a way he still could not explain.

But that doesn't change the fact that I died — I died! he thought, as he strained against the Rahkshi. *Is that a possibility I can face again?*

The metallic mouth of the Rahkshi opened to reveal the slimy kraata slug inside. The repulsive sight brought more memories. The village of Ta-Koro destroyed . . . Ko-Koro badly damaged . . . Matoran fleeing for their lives . . . all because of these monsters.

"Never again!" Jaller shouted, wrenching

himself free of the Rahkshi's grasp. He aimed his energized flame sword, intending to create a wall of flame between him and his opponent. The fires appeared, as he had wished, but something immediately went wrong. The lightning refused to stay intertwined with the flames, instead lancing out in all directions. One bolt struck the Rahkshi, instantly destroying the kraata inside.

The Rahkshi armor collapsed to the ground. Jaller stared down at his handiwork, feeling just as empty as the scorched metal exo-skeleton at his feet.

By the time Kongu had gotten into position, Hewkii had trashed his Bohrok foe, Nuparu was locked in combat with a Bohrok-Kal, and Matoro was trying to ice the wings of the Nui-Rama. Strangely enough, neither the Kal nor Makuta had said anything during the battle.

Usually we can't get these losers to shut up, Kongu thought.

"Not sure how you got this monster-crew together, Makuta," the Toa Inika of Air said. "But it won't do you any good. We're going quick-down those stairs, around you or over you — your choice."

Makuta did not reply, his silence infuriating Kongu. The Toa took aim with his energy cross-bow and fired two bolts. Makuta made no effort to get out of the way. Instead, he simply waved his hand and the two bursts of energy froze in midair. Then the bolts dropped, hit the floor, and shattered like glass.

Undeterred, Kongu called upon his power over air, creating a mini-cyclone centered on Makuta. The winds were so powerful that noth-ing could breathe within, or stay rooted to the ground. Yet somehow Makuta remained unaffected. In fact, the power of the master of shadows cut right through the cyclone to blast Kongu with solid darkness.

The Toa of Air picked himself painfully up off the stairs. Something was not right here. The Mask of Telepathy he wore should have been picking up a morass of evil thoughts from Makuta, but nothing was coming through, from him or from any of the other foes. Even stranger, Makuta had taken everything he had to throw at him without as much as a scratch.

Well, not everything, Kongu reminded himself. *I still have this zamor sphere launcher. But zamors loaded with energized protodermis wouldn't just stop him . . . they'd kill him.*

He toyed with the thought for an instant. Makuta had been tormenting the Matoran for centuries. He had driven them from Metru Nui to Mata Nui, and even then did everything he could to keep them living in fear and despair.

He might ever-deserve to die, thought Kongu. *But if I kill him in ice-cold blood, I'm no better than he is . . . and not worthy of being a Toa-hero.*

Suddenly, the choice was no longer Kongu's to make. His launcher fired on its own, sending the sphere straight at Makuta. It struck the master of shadows dead on. Makuta screamed as the bizarre substance began dissolving his armor.

"No!" yelled Kongu, rushing to the side of his fallen enemy. "How is this possible? I didn't fire!"

It was too late for questions. Makuta was dead, slain by the Toa Inika of Air. And Kongu knew that nothing could ever be the same again.

The battle was over.

The Toa Inika's six opponents were stretched out on the stone steps. All of them were dead, and none of the Toa was quite sure how it had happened. They had not set out to kill any of their enemies, nor been forced into it by circumstance. It had just . . . happened.

"We lost control," said Hahli, sadly. "All this power . . . maybe it is too much for us to handle."

"It was just bad luck," said Hewkii. "That's all it was."

"Bad luck for us. Worse luck for them," said Kongu, bending over to inspect the damaged Bohrok and its dead krana. "None of which explains what a Bohrok and a Bohrok-Kal were even doing here, when we know they shouldn't be. I — hey!"

The outer surface of the Bohrok began to

shimmer and fade. As it did so, another form came into view. The sight stole the breath from Kongu's lungs.

"It's Pohatu Nuva!" he cried. "This Bohrok . . . it just turned into Pohatu Nuva!"

The other Toa Inika rushed over. The same thing was happening to all of their fallen foes. Makuta had transformed into Tahu Nuva, the Rahkshi into Kopaka Nuva, the Muaka to Onua Nuva, the Nui-Rama into Lewa Nuva, and the Bohrok-Kal into Gali Nuva. All six were there, and all six were dead at the hands of the Toa Inika.

"Illusions," whispered Toa Jaller. "We fought illusions of our greatest enemies, never knowing . . . and when we struck, we killed our friends."

Toa Hewkii threw his zamor launcher and laser axe on the ground and walked away. "We were tricked into murdering them! Someone knew we were just stupid enough to believe whatever we saw, and they used us!"

"That's not even the worst of it," said

Matoro. "How can we trust our senses, or ourselves, after this? If we can't tell friend from enemy, if we can't control our powers, we're not heroes . . . we're menaces."

"So what do you want us to do?" Kongu said, anger in his voice. "Give up? Hope some other Toa-heroes come along in time to save the Great Spirit?"

Nuparu sat down on the stairs and stared at the ground. "But, Kongu, how could we be sure we *were* saving him? What if . . . what if we got tricked again and we killed Mata Nui? Are you prepared to risk causing the death of the universe?"

An uncomfortable silence descended on the six Toa. All of them, at one point or another, had worried that the power they now wielded might be too much to bear. It was impossible to go from being Matoran one moment to Toa the next, without having such fears. But none had ever dreamed the misuse of their energies would lead to such a disaster.

"I don't see what choice we have," said

Hahli. "If we can't rely on our judgment, and we are afraid of our power, we can't be effective. We can't accomplish our mission. Jaller, we will have to turn back."

The Toa Inika of Fire didn't answer. His eyes were locked on the unmoving form of Tahu Nuva. When he spoke, his voice was ragged with grief. "Tahu told me something once, not long after he first arrived on our island. He said having real courage doesn't mean being unafraid of death — it means you keep on striving for what's right despite your fear."

He looked up at his partners. "Don't you see? The Toa risked death every single day against Makuta, the Rahkshi, the Bohrok. They knew something like this might happen and they kept on fighting anyway. They weren't perfect — they made mistakes, they fought with each other — but they kept going, and they would expect the same of us."

"Even after this?" asked Hahli quietly.

"Especially after this," Jaller replied. "Because it means we are on our own, with no hope of aid." When no one spoke, he added, "I am going on, in honor of Tahu Nuva's memory and Lhikan's memory and all the other Toa who came before us. Who else will join me?"

One by one, each of the Toa Inika stepped forward. With a last look at their fallen heroes, they turned to resume their journey. They had gone only a few steps when Toa Hewkii paused to look back. What he saw — or rather, didn't see — stunned him.

"They're gone! The Toa Nuva have disappeared!"

The Inika rushed to the spot where the dead Toa had been lying. There was no trace of them.

"We only had our backs turned for a second," said Hahli. "What could have happened?"

"Well, they didn't get up and walk away," said Matoro, adding quickly, "I hope."

"You are blind-missing a better question: what if they were never here at all?" Kongu replied. He tapped the side of his mask. "Kanohi Suletu, remember? Telepathy. All thoughts, all the time. But I picked up nothing but ever-silence from those six."

"And no thoughts means no minds," said Hewkii.

"And no minds means they were just illusions," concluded Kongu. Then he added, smiling, "Or else they were all Po-Matoran."

Matoro grinned. Hahli tried in vain to stifle a giggle. Seconds later, the ancient staircase was ringing with a living, vibrant sound it had not experienced in its entire history: laughter.

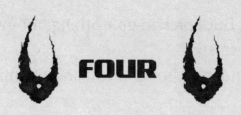

FOUR

The Piraka were not amused.

Their journey had been brought to an abrupt halt in a most disturbing way. Six cylinders of stone had erupted from the staircase, trapping each of them in their own individual prison. The stone rapidly proved too smooth to climb and impervious to eyebeams, brute strength, or Piraka weaponry. Although the cylinders were open at the top, Zaktan's attempt to fly out was met by a jolt of electricity sufficient to send him crashing back to earth.

All of the cylinders shared one feature in common. On the inside of each, at roughly waist level, was a stone latch. Just why it was there was a mystery, as there were no visible signs of a door.

"What's next?" grumbled Thok. "The walls close in? Swarms of fireflyers attack? The Shadowed One sings?"

Inferno

His answer didn't come from any of the other Piraka, but from an aged voice that boomed from all around them. Although none of the captives knew it, the voice belonged to the Great Being who had crafted the route to the Mask of Life. The words had been spoken thousands of years before.

"Travelers, you now face another test," the voice said. "Only two types of being can escape the cylinders in which you find yourselves — the completely selfless, and the completely selfish.

"Behold the latches in your prison cells. If all of you raise your latches at the same time, then the cylinders will open and you are free to proceed. All will be well, and all will have an equal chance to obtain the Mask of Life. But if one of you raises his latch before the others do, he and only he will be free to continue on his way, while all of his companions will be destroyed. You must decide."

Zaktan immediately shouted, "No one touches their latch!"

Thok pulled his hand back from the piece

of stone as if he had been burned. "All right, Zaktan, you don't have to yell! We're trapped, not deaf."

"Avak, have you found another way out of these cylinders?" asked Zaktan.

"No, and if there's one thing I know, it's prison cells," Avak replied. "It looks like the voice was telling the truth — it's all of us . . . or only one of us."

"Then I suppose we have to . . . work together," Hakann said, the words obviously disgusting him.

"Exactly, and quickly," Zaktan answered. He knew the more time his teammates had to think, the better the chance one of them would betray the rest. It had certainly crossed his mind, but going on alone would be madness. *Partners are necessary so that future opponents will have someone to demolish while I escape,* he reasoned.

"Then at the count of three, we all raise our latches at once," said Avak. "Are we agreed?"

Each of the Piraka said yes. Zaktan wasn't

sure which worried him more — that Hakann was the first to answer or Vezok the last.

"1 . . . 2 . . ."

Suddenly, the floor opened up beneath all six Piraka. A powerful suction drew them down to a fate unknown. As they slid through narrow stone channels, Reidak could be heard shouting, "He lied! The voice lied!"

Their unexpected journey ended with a splash. The Piraka flew out the end of the passages and right into a large pool of liquid protodermis. They plunged far beneath it, but fortunately, its depth was great enough that they did not strike the bottom. When they broke the surface again, all of them were unharmed . . . at least, for the moment.

"Reidak!" Zaktan shouted in a rage. "You moron! Of course he lied! The whole thing was a trap for any team that could not trust each other. The second you raised that latch and tried to betray us, you doomed us all."

"Don't blame Reidak — maybe he wasn't

trying to cross us. Maybe he just can't count," commented Avak. He looked around. "And, hey, this isn't bad, as dooms go."

He had a point. The liquid protodermis was actually refreshing after the long climb down the stairs. Granted there didn't seem to be any easy way to get out of it. The water filled the entire chamber and the only exits were the passages the Piraka had slid down, entrances to which were on the ceiling high above. But the Piraka had escaped from worse traps in their time.

"We will discuss this later," Zaktan said, in a tone that left no doubt the conversation would not be a pleasant one for Reidak. "Let's get out of here."

Zaktan dissolved his body into a free-floating mass of protodites and began to rise into the air. He had made it only a few feet above the water when slabs of stone started falling away from the walls all over the chamber. The Piraka dove under the water as the rocks struck, sending huge splashes into the air. When the hail of rock was done, there were dozens and dozens of recessed slots exposed in the walls.

There was a moment of uneasy silence. The Piraka returned to the surface, their eyes darting around to see what would happen next. They didn't have long to wait. Jets of white-hot flame erupted from each slot, forming fiery "bars" above the water. Zaktan yelled in pain and dropped back into the pool.

Reidak squinted at the bright glow. The air above the water was now a mass of fire and the Piraka were caged just as surely as if they had been in a cell.

"Now what?" said Avak.

"Maybe they aren't really there," suggested Thok. "Like Irnakk."

"Let's throw Reidak up there and find out," said Hakann.

"They are real enough," hissed Zaktan. "I lost enough protodites to know that."

"Okay, so we stay in the water," said Vezok, "until the flame jets run out of power."

Thok looked at his partner as if Vezok had just grown a second head. "What happens to water when it's exposed to flame?"

In the old days, Vezok would have shot back the answer in an instant. Since he had been split into two beings — himself and Vezon — he had not been quite so swift. He paused for a moment, wondering if this might be a trick question, before saying, "It boils?"

"And so do we, if we stay here," said Thok. "Or we could try climbing the walls to reach the exits and get fried. Take your pick."

The only answer came from the flame jets, which suddenly increased in power. Soon, the Piraka knew, they would be forced under the water, which would add drowning to their list of possible fates.

"That settles it," said Hakann. "Next time someone invites me to join a group, I'm saying no."

FIVE

Velika stood before the doorway to a narrow passage leading downward. He looked puzzled. "The mountain can be shaped by rain and wind . . . but can the mountain shape itself by drive and will?"

"Will someone please tell him to stop that?" muttered Kazi.

Balta went to stand beside the Po-Matoran. "No, he's found something. Remember, Velika oversaw the team of Matoran who built this fortress for the Piraka. He knows every corner of it. If he says this wasn't there before, then it wasn't. The Piraka must have carved out a lower level."

The Matoran rushed down the passage, heedless of any traps that might be waiting. If the Toa Nuva were still alive, every moment that passed could place them in terrible danger.

"Down here!" Balta shouted. He had found a chamber sealed by a door made of stone three feet thick. An iron ring served as a handle, but it would take someone with the strength of Reidak to open it.

Garan turned to Kazi. "We'll work together. The rest of you, back off."

The Onu-Matoran and the Ko-Matoran prepared themselves for their task. Then both raised their weapons and fired, Garan launching a pulse bolt and Kazi a blast of sonics. Despite its strength, the chamber door could not stand up to this double bombardment. With a sound like thunder, it shattered into rubble.

Balta did not even wait for the dust to clear before scrambling over the stone. He could make out six figures, maskless, chained to the wall. Elemental energies flowed from their hands into a bottomless well in the center of the room. They looked drained and exhausted, and their eyes glowed with a faint red gleam.

"Incredible," Balta said. "They must have been enslaved by the virus and imprisoned here.

Whoever did it ordered them to pour their ele-mental energies out until there was no more, and then go beyond that point."

Piruk and Velika set to work breaking the chains. The Toa Nuva did not respond, seeming to take no notice of the fact that anyone had come into the chamber.

"Even if they fought off the effects of the virus, they would have had no power left to escape," said Garan. "And who knows what else might have happened? The constant drain might even have killed them over time."

All six Toa Nuva were free — physically, at least. Now the Matoran had to free them from mental enslavement as well. Each loaded his launcher with one of the same zamor spheres the Toa Inika had used to free the Matoran pop-ulation of the island.

"Fire!" said Garan.

The spheres struck their targets. All six Toa Nuva immediately slumped to the ground, as if struck dead. Dalu rushed to Tahu Nuva, only to find he was still alive, just badly weakened.

"Wake up!" she urged. "The Toa Inika need you!"

"Your tools are here. We can take you to your masks," Balta said, helping Kopaka Nuva to rise. "I just hope it is not already too late."

"Toa . . . Inika?" asked Onua Nuva. "What . . . what are you talking about?"

"It's a long story," said Garan. "We'll tell you on the way."

Hakann looked up at the burning bars of flame, now not so very far overhead. "So how do we like our Piraka," he asked, "baked or boiled?"

"Be quiet," said Zaktan. "I'm thinking."

"Oh, then I'll alert a Chronicler," the crimson-armored Piraka said sarcastically. "Your thinking is what brought us here. As I recall, you thought looting Makuta's corpse would be a grand idea."

Zaktan ignored him. "We can't go forward, back, or up. That leaves down. Vezok, dive deep and see what you can find."

Grateful to get away from the awful heat,

Vezok complied. As he went farther down, the water cooled to a more comfortable temperature. The whole thing seemed like a Matoran's errand to him, though, since it was so dark at the pool's bottom, he could not see a thing. Determined to find a way out, he began feeling his way along the floor, looking for some kind of a gap.

There! He had chanced upon a narrow opening between two rocks. A few quick blows widened it a little, just enough for someone his size to fit through. Then he went back to get the others, so that no matter what might be waiting in the tunnel, Reidak would be going first.

Moments later, all six Piraka were swimming through the gap. Beyond it was a winding tunnel that went down, then up, then veered sharply down again, then settled into a long, gentle ascent. There was barely enough room to move, let alone fight back if anything attacked.

Bringing up the rear, Hakann was the one who noticed that stone slabs were falling into place behind them as they swam. There would be no going back if they didn't like their destination.

Reidak suddenly stopped swimming and pointed upward. Then he vanished into the ceiling. It was only when Hakann got a little closer that he realized there was another tunnel branching off this one and heading straight up. He followed his partners into it, hoping it led somewhere with breathable air.

To his great relief, it did. The Piraka emerged on a vast plain of hardened magma. At the far edge, a huge stone bridge spanned a river of lava. The far tower of the bridge featured a small gateway at the bottom. Instinctively, the Piraka knew they had almost reached their goal. So excited were they that none of them noticed the subtle, minute changes already happening to them due to their exposure to the water. But there would be time enough to realize, and tremble, later.

"Let's go," said Thok. "The mask must be close now."

"Wait," ordered Zaktan. The Piraka looked back at him in surprise. "I want the Mask of Life as well, but I don't want to have to fight my way past six Toa to escape with it. They may be close behind — it will cost us nothing to set a trap for them here, and then take the mask at our leisure."

Hakann frowned. Zaktan had been the one pushing hardest to find the mask from the beginning, and now he wanted to wait? Then again, if the other five Piraka and the Toa Inika destroyed each other in battle, Zaktan could claim the mask for himself with no opposition.

Regardless, the Piraka leader was right. If the Toa surprised them in a confined space when they had to worry about protecting the mask, they would be demolished. Better to choose the battle site themselves.

"Then let's get to work," said Hakann. "There's nothing like an ambush to brighten up your day."

At the moment, fighting the Piraka was the furthest thing from the Toa's minds. They had come to yet another chamber along the stairway's path, this one lit by dark red lightstones. Although there were no enemies visible, something about the room felt wrong. The Toa advanced with caution.

"Welcome, travelers," a voice boomed from every side. The Toa's eyes scanned the chamber but saw no one. "You seek the Chamber of Life . . . but first you must pass through the Chamber of Death, for truly both are intertwined."

"Come out where we can see you!" shouted Jaller.

The voice ignored him. "For millennia beyond count, the Mask of Life has been hidden in this place, waiting for destiny's call. It is a Kanohi both wonderful and terrible in its might. And the price to wield its power of life . . . is death."

"Well, that is happy-cheerful," muttered Kongu. "You take us to the nicest places, Jaller, old friend."

"Six of you stand ready," the voice continued. "If you wish to pass through this chamber, one of you must die. Decide — now."

"And what if we choose not to abide by your rules?" said Hahli. "What if we fight?"

Again, the voice ignored all argument, merely repeating its last statement. The Toa's response was to charge for the exit on the other side of the chamber, only to find themselves blocked by an invisible barrier. It reminded Jaller of the one that had cut him off from Toa Takanuva on the journey to Voya Nui, but there was no time to consider the implications of that.

"We go back," said the Toa Inika of Fire. "We'll find another way down, or make one."

He turned around, just in time to see a massive stone slab come down, cutting off their exit. It proved to be impervious to his fire, as well as Matoro's ice and even Hewkii's power over rock. The Toa were trapped.

The voice spoke again. "Two choices have you — renounce your pursuit of the Mask of Life, and you may leave as you came, never to return. Or choose one of your number to die, so that the rest may pass. There are no other pathways open to your tread."

Jaller considered. He had no idea where the Piraka were or whether they might already have found the mask. There seemed no way out of this chamber, and renouncing the quest would result in who knows what — maybe even some kind of sudden transport back to Metru Nui and utter failure. No, there really was no choice. He was the leader of the Toa Inika, so if someone had to be sacrificed, it should be him.

He started to speak, but somehow the words caught in his throat. He had a sudden flash of memory of the day he died at the claws of the Rahkshi. The recollection was so vivid that it froze Jaller for a split second. It was the sound of another voice that freed him from his paralysis.

"I volunteer," said Matoro, stepping forward. "If someone has to die, let it be me."

"Matoro! No!" cried Hahli.

"Absolutely not," said Jaller, taken completely by surprise. He addressed the mysterious voice, saying, "Whoever you are, this is not our choice!"

"Yes, we have gotten ever-used to frosty here," added Kongu.

Matoro turned to his friends. "Please. This is the logical choice. I'm not a warrior, like you, Jaller, or you, Kongu — or an athlete, or an inventor, or even a Chronicler. I am just a translator for a Turaga, and not even that anymore. I won't save the universe with my fists or my wits, but maybe I can do it this way."

"Matoro, you don't have to —" Jaller began.

"The choice has been made," the voice said, cutting off the Toa leader. "The price will be paid."

Before any of the Toa could protest, a beam of light shone down on Matoro. In a millisecond, his body had dissolved, leaving only his mask hovering in the shaft of illumination. Then that too faded away.

For a moment, there was silence, broken only by the muffled sobbing of Toa Hahli. Then something akin to dust began to swirl inside the light. It rotated faster and faster, until it began to take on definite form. A moment later, that form became recognizable as Matoro's Kanohi mask.

Now more and more sparkling particles appeared, twisting and melding together inside the beam. None of the Toa dared speak lest they disturb the stunning event they were witnessing. Before their eyes, Matoro's body was reforming, whole and undamaged, as if it had never been gone at all.

When the process was complete, the light disappeared. Toa Matoro looked around in confusion, but what he felt could not begin to equal the emotions in the hearts of his friends.

"It is done," said the voice. "This one has died and been reborn, and so the price is paid . . . the debt is settled. For it is not the cold fact of death that matters, but the willingness to die for one's cause. This one had the courage to accept destruction so that his comrades could live, so final death will not be his this day."

The stone slab that blocked the staircase behind the Toa was gone. A shimmer in the air told them the force barrier had vanished as well.

"You are free to pass on," said the voice.

The Toa did not hesitate. They proceeded through the exit and down the stairs — and as they resumed their journey, it was not lost on Jaller that Matoro had taken the lead.

The next several minutes of the journey were quiet ones, giving each Toa Inika some time to reflect. There were still so many questions to be answered. What had happened to the Toa Nuva? Assuming those veteran heroes were safe, what then? Would they want the Inika to return to Metru Nui and watch over the city with Takanuva? After so much action and adventure, what would it be like to have to settle for simple guard duty?

Their pondering was interrupted by a sound from farther down the staircase, one that resembled the scream of a Muaka mixed with the angry buzzing of a very large Nui-Rama.

"Oh, good," said Kongu. "We haven't had to hard-fight for our lives in at least two minutes."

They moved on cautiously, scanning the walls for any niches or caverns from which the sound might have emanated. They didn't see anything suspicious until they reached a wider chamber — and then they saw nothing at all, as all the lightstones embedded in the walls exploded simultaneously. Jaller activated his flame sword in time to see clawed figures dropping down from the ceiling.

"Watch out!" he shouted. As the first creature dropped near him, the light of his flame revealed it to be a two-headed beast with a lizard-like tail. It stood on two legs, and its forelegs ended in razor-sharp talons. Jaller swung his sword and struck the monster. To his amazement, it did not go down, but rather split into two beings, both just as big and powerful as the original. The other Toa were making the same discovery, as their six attackers had now multiplied into twelve.

The Toa backed up the stairs, with Hewkii using his powers to create a wall of rock between them and their foes. It provided temporary protection but also kept the Toa from advancing any farther toward the Mask of Life.

Without bothering to wait for Jaller to ask, Kongu used his Mask of Telepathy to probe the creatures' minds. There wasn't much there that was coherent, but enough that he could say, "They're not intelligent beings. They're . . . Jaller, they're protodites!"

"That's crazy," said Hewkii. "Protodites are microscopic in size. These things are bigger than we are!"

"The Mask of Life," replied Hahli. "Do you think its power could have —"

Her question was interrupted by the shattering of Hewkii's wall. The creatures charged, and Hewkii and Nuparu lashed out by reflex. The next thing anyone knew, there were sixteen of the ravenous beasts.

"Remember that time I was hanging upside down in a swamp hole, just above some hungry mud crawlers," said Nuparu. "You know, the ones with the acidic tongues and the breath that smells like Tarakava that's been out in the sun too long?"

"Sure, what about it?" answered Kongu.

Nuparu sighed. "Those were the good old days, huh?"

Then the creatures were upon them, clawing and scratching, while the Toa tried desperately to fight them off without striking and making more of them. Elemental powers proved some help in this, but even the most optimistic of the Toa could tell they were fighting a losing battle — and the darkness only made it worse.

A sudden flash of light temporarily blinded the Toa. They heard a rush of wind and then more bursts of light filled the stairway. The creatures screamed and scattered, their weak eyes unused to the bright glare. For just a moment, Jaller found himself hoping that Takanuva, the Toa of Light, had somehow made it to Voya Nui.

When his vision cleared, he discovered he could not have been more wrong. The yellow-armored being who stood on the stairs holding a wicked staff could not have been further from his friend. Jaller's eyes were drawn to the figure's feet, which featured rounded devices that looked something like gears. The Toa of Fire could not recall seeing anyone actually standing on their gears before, though. The figure regarded the assembled Toa with cold, empty eyes — and then he was gone.

No, not gone, Jaller realized, as he felt something fly past him. *Just moving too fast for the eye to see.*

The Toa whirled, trying to catch a glimpse of their new foe. He was riding on the walls at an incredible rate of speed, leaping the gaps to circle the heroes. Toa Kongu raised his crossbow, only to have it shot out of his hand by a thin laser beam fired by the yellow blur crisscrossing the room.

"Slow him down," Jaller said to Hewkii. The Toa Inika of Stone used his power to make sharp, angular rocks jut out from the walls. But the figure maneuvered around them with ease, never slowing long enough for anyone to have a clear target.

"I've had enough of this," snapped Kongu, unleashing a lightning-laced tornado at the far wall. It was big enough to totally block the figure's path and powerful enough to fling him the length of the chamber if he got caught in it.

The enemy's speed slackened only a fraction as he approached the violently rotating column of air. Then he shot off the wall straight at Kongu, his momentum carrying him over the Toa. His wheeled feet clipped Kongu's head, knocking the Toa of Air to the ground.

"That does it!" said Kongu, scrambling to his feet. "I've been beaten, sharp-clawed, stone-grabbed, and Piraka-pounded — but that does it! I hope this Rahi-breath has his memorial stone carved already, because he's going to need it."

The figure had skidded to a halt between the Toa and the chamber's far exit. Its expression had not changed. When it spoke, its voice was as cold as a kraata's heart. "I am Umbra. I guard the Mask of Life. You shall not pass."

"This makes no sense," Hahli said. "First you save us from those . . . things, and now you want to fight us. Why?"

"The protodax are violent beasts," Umbra replied. "They do not kill with honor — they simply kill. I leave to them the simpleminded Rahi who accidentally wander down this far, but those with heart and spirit are mine to destroy."

"Another threat," said Hewkii. "Is there anyone on this crummy island who doesn't make threats?"

"Insanity," said Hahli. "How can a mere Kanohi mask be worth so many lives?"

"If you do not know its worth," Umbra replied, "then why are you here?"

With that, Umbra rocketed forward again. In a millisecond, he had disarmed all six Toa and filled Hewkii with a hundred blows delivered between one breath and the next.

"Okay, if he's doing all the race-running, why am I the one who's deep-tired?" asked Kongu.

"And how come there's never a Mask of Time around when you need one?" added Nuparu.

Matoro smiled. "We're looking at this the wrong way. Forget about slowing him down — let's speed him up."

The Toa Inika of Ice concentrated, sending waves of cold throughout the chamber. The walls, ceiling and floor began to ice over. In a matter of moments, they were dangerously slick, a fact Umbra found out. Following the curve of the left-hand wall, he suddenly skidded out of control and crashed hard to the floor.

"Slam-bang," said Kongu, cheerfully. "I like it."

"He's down. He's not out," warned Jaller. "It's going to take more than a little ice to stop him."

As if on cue, Umbra began to shift and change. Before the Toa's startled eyes, he changed from a physical being to a concentrated beam of light. Jaller just managed to push Nuparu out of the way before the laser-like Umbra struck him. Their foe's light form melted a hole in the back wall, then shot back toward the Toa.

"Down!" Jaller yelled. This new attack was even worse than Umbra's super-speed — at least before, he had a physical body and could be struck if one could catch up to him. *How do we fight a beam of light?*

The answer came as Umbra shot past overhead multiple times in a second. Jaller was only slightly annoyed to realize the key was Matoro.

"We need more ice," he shouted. "Block the exits. And it needs to be like polished crystal!"

Without any urging, Hahli used her power to create more moisture for Matoro to work with. He rapidly covered the Toa and Umbra with a dome of freezing cold, crystalline ice. As soon as this was done, it was Nuparu's turn. He triggered the power of his mask and flew toward the far wall, as if making a break for the iced-over exit leading to the location of the mask.

Umbra did just what Jaller expected: he flashed after Nuparu in light form. Just before reaching the wall, Nuparu cut off his mask's energies and dropped to the stone floor. Umbra kept going, his light beam striking and then bouncing off the reflective ice. The ricochet carried him to another wall of ice, where he reflected again. Then he was flashing all over the chamber, bouncing back and forth by the mirror-bright ice. Finally, it was too much even for Umbra to take and he reappeared in physical, and unconscious, form on the floor.

The Toa Inika wasted no time. Jaller recovered his energized flame sword and used it to cut a hole in the ice covering the exit. Then he and the others rushed down another few dozen stairs and onto a volcanic plain.

After so long in the narrow stairway, broken up only by the occasional stone chamber, the vastness of the plain was disconcerting. Nuparu did a fast fly-over of the bridge in the distance and returned to report that the Piraka were already positioned there.

"How are you with bridges?" Kongu asked.

"Watch me," Nuparu, Toa Inika of Earth, replied.

The earthquake that followed lasted only for a few seconds, but it was long enough to shake half the Piraka off their posts. Once their foes were off balance, the Toa charged. Zaktan,

Hakann, and Thok rained zamor spheres down on them, and the Toa responded with bursts of elemental power.

Times like this, I could use a Mask of Shielding, thought Jaller. *Before all is said and done, I am going to get my old mask back — the one Karzahni took from me — even if I have to go back there by myself. It dishonors Toa Lhikan's memory to just let it be lost. Plus, I am really, really tired of dodging.*

Despite his concerns, the battle was going the Toa's way. Thok and Hakann had already abandoned their positions, and Hahli, Hewkii, and Nuparu were keeping three of the Piraka too busy to strike back. Only Zaktan was still manning a hastily constructed launcher and refusing all efforts to dislodge him.

That's when Kongu got his idea. Zaktan was made out of billions of microscopic protodites — and little things tend not to like big winds. A well-placed cyclone might disperse the Piraka leader and clear the way for a Toa victory. For a fast mover like the Toa Inika of Air, thought was deed, and his cyclone was on its way. Unfortunately, the sound of rushing wind drowned out Jaller and Matoro's calls for him to stop.

The funnel of air smashed into Zaktan, sending his protodites flying in multiple directions. But the bridge, already weakened by Nuparu's earthquake, could not stand up to the punishing winds. It groaned, twisted, and collapsed, burying the Toa underneath it. The Piraka, having been driven away from the bridge before the collapse, fared better. They were already assembled when Zaktan managed to regain control of his component parts and get back on the ground.

"Let us hope the Toa have fallen for the last time," Zaktan said. "Come, let's go. The Mask of Life is waiting."

The five Piraka followed him, broad grins on their faces as they contemplated the end of their quest. Those smiles might have been erased had they known that something else besides the mask — something powerful, evil, and quite mad — was waiting for them beyond the gateway.

* * *

The door at the base of the bridge opened onto a huge chamber bordered on three sides by lava channels. But that was not what left the Piraka gaping, openmouthed. Rather, it was the caped figure who dominated the room from atop a giant Rahi spider. His identity should not have been a surprise, yet somehow it was.

"Vezon," Zaktan said softly.

"Vezon," Vezok repeated, with barely contained rage.

"How convenient," said the rider. "You know my name . . . and of course I know yours . . . and isn't it only right that you should spend your last moments of life with an old, dear friend?"

SIX

Vezon yanked hard on the chain he held. In response, the head of the giant spider he rode jerked up. The creature bared its multiple vicious fangs and gave a savage hiss. It crawled a few paces toward the assembled Piraka, its red eyes glaring fiercely at them. There was something revolting about its every movement.

"You're early," said Vezon. "Or are you late? I never can keep those two straight . . . not that it matters very much, down here. Had a little problem with the Matoran, did we?"

"You were up there?" asked Thok, never taking his eyes off Vezon's monstrous mount.

"I was down here," Vezon corrected. "Way, way down here. But the mask knew you were coming. . . . It knew, you see, and that's why it wanted me. That's why it introduced me to Fenrakk here, and told us to wait very quietly

74

until you arrived." An evil gleam sprang to life in Vezon's eyes. "So you see, whatever happens to you next, you brought on yourselves."

Zaktan detached a small portion of the microscopic protodites that made up his body and sent them flying silently to scout the chamber. But his efforts did not go unnoticed. Vezon's eyes darted in the direction of the motion. Energy poured from his spear, striking the protodites and fusing them together into a solid mass. The fused creatures hit the floor, dead.

"Pests," Vezon said. "It's so hard to keep an underground lava chamber free of pests."

Avak had already had enough. He called upon his power and summoned a cage to surround Vezon and Fenrakk. It took only an instant for the two to be safely behind bars that could resist even their combined powers.

"Oh, very good," said Vezon, smiling happily. "But you see, Avak, I am already in prison. You have just shown me the bars. And you can't get what you want if I am in here."

The deranged Piraka threw his head back

and laughed. As he did so, Zaktan saw that a Kanohi mask was fused to the back of his skull. A glance at the empty pedestal in the rear of the chamber told him all he needed to know. "You're wearing the Mask of Life," the emerald-armored Piraka said.

"Wearing it, cursed by it, serving it, raging at it," Vezon replied. "Not always in that order. Want it? Come try and take it. Please."

Reidak took a step toward the cage. Fenrakk snapped at him, barely missing the Piraka's hand. Slime oozed from the spider's mouth. Every drop that hit the stone floor produced a sizzling sound and a wisp of smoke.

"Then it's a stand-off," said Zaktan.

"A stand-off," Vezon repeated.

"We can't get at the mask . . . and you can't get at us."

Vezon said nothing.

"We have to make some arrangement."

"An arrangement," Vezon agreed.

"What do you want for the mask?" asked Zaktan.

Fenrakk backed away from the bars, carrying Vezon back into the shadows. Only the mad Piraka's crimson eyes were visible as he said, "What do I want? What do I need? I have so much — eternal life; the loyalty, devotion, and companionship of a monstrous killing machine; all the lava eels I can eat. What could you possibly offer? What service could you possibly perform?"

A pause. Then Vezon's expression brightened. "Ah, I know! You could kill Vezok!"

"Let me in there!" Vezok shouted. "I'll strangle that freak and shove that spear down his —"

Reidak grabbed his partner and flung him hard against the stone wall. Before Vezok could react, Thok's ice weapon had covered him with a thick sheet of ice. Hakann followed that up with a mental blast that shattered Vezok's thoughts into a million shards.

"A few more of those and he won't be a problem for anyone anymore," Hakann said to Vezon. "The Spear of Fusion, used in reverse, split you off from Vezok, and you don't want to risk being joined back up with him . . . am I warm?"

"Searing," Vezon replied.

"We do this, and we get the mask?"

"You do that," Vezon answered, "and we'll talk."

Hakann turned back to Vezok. He was greeted by an explosion of ice. The next moment, both he and Reidak were being slammed by mental blasts, courtesy of Vezok's ability to copy the powers of others. Hakann tried to scramble away. Vezok grabbed him by the spine, spun him around, and threw him at Zaktan. The Piraka leader naturally dodged, allowing Hakann to slam headfirst into a stone wall.

"You're going to believe him?" Vezok bellowed, pointing at Vezon. "I can understand murderous . . . I can even deal with treacherous . . . but you five are just stupid!"

Vezon giggled. "You left out 'highly entertaining,' Vezok."

"You couldn't give us the mask if you wanted to, could you?" said Vezok.

Vezon shook his head. "You will have to pry it off my cold, dead head. That's part of the curse. When I came down here . . . when I dared try to take the mask . . . it fused itself to me, just as it fused me to Fenrakk here."

"Let him out of the cage," Vezok said to Avak.

"Are you crazy?" Avak answered. "You may want to face that lunatic and his pet spider, but I don't."

Vezok turned, grabbed Avak, slammed him onto the stone floor, and pinned him there. "Let him . . . OUT . . . of the cage! I'll tear the mask off him!" When Avak hesitated, Vezok used a borrowed mental blast to knock him unconscious. The cage around Vezon disappeared.

Vezok stalked toward his enemy. "Now, you misshapen mockery of a Piraka, we'll settle things once and for all. Then I'll rip the Spear of Fusion out of your claws and use it to put you back in me, where you belong!"

"The Spear of Fusion?" Vezon repeated, as if in a daze. Then he looked down at the weapon he held, muttering, "That's right, I do have that, don't I?" A beam of energy shot out from the tip of the spear, bathing Vezok and Reidak in its power. Instantly, the two of them were fused together into a lumbering, skull-faced giant.

Vezon looked at his creation and was satisfied. Gesturing dismissively at the other Piraka, he said, "Kill them."

The newly formed creature moved to obey. Born from two Piraka, it was twice as eager to grind its enemies into dust and then blow the dust away.

"You know," said Toa Hewkii, "I'm getting really tired of losing to those guys . . . even when it's our own fault."

Hahli sat on the ground, cradling her head in both hands. The proximity of the Mask of Life was making her head feel like it was going to split open.

"It's our own fault," said Toa Jaller, standing up amidst the rubble. "We keep fighting like

Matoran, trying to be honorable and merciful the way the Turaga and the Toa Nuva taught us."

"Against the Piraka, we might as well be wearing signs that say, 'Stomp us,'" Kongu muttered.

"Then let's tear the signs off," said Matoro. "I agree with Hewkii — I'm sick of winding up flat on my mask."

"Let's go," said Jaller, marching toward the gate. "And when we find them, we fight hard and we fight dirty. The Piraka have a long history of beating Toa — well, it stops with us!"

Brutaka met Axonn's charge with one of his own. Just before they were going to collide, Axonn sidestepped and hit Brutaka with the flat of his axe. His foe went sprawling.

Axonn had no time to enjoy his victory, though, for the dimensional vortex was still closing in. He grabbed his axe and swung it at the floating portal. Energy flashed from the weapon, driving the vortex back.

"Is this what we've come to?" Axonn said, fighting to get his breath back. "Clawing at each other like a pair of maddened Rahi?"

Brutaka fired a blast from his sword, knocking Axonn back toward the vortex. "Yes," he answered. "Rahi beasts are all that we are — it's all anyone is. And when we're done, I will be the most powerful beast in the jungle."

Axonn's eyes narrowed. Despite all that had happened, all that Brutaka had done, he had never realized just how badly lost his old friend had become.

"I tried," he said, sadness and anger mixing in his voice. "I hoped that I could still reach some part of you, Brutaka, some remnant of the hero you used to be. But that being is dead. Maybe he died when you met the Piraka, or the contents of that crystal vat . . . or maybe he was dead long before then, and I simply never noticed."

Axonn started walking toward his former friend. Brutaka responded with another blast of energy. Axonn ignored the impact and the pain and kept going. "I deny you," he said.

Brutaka fired again, this time with enough force to bring down a Kanohi Dragon. Again, impossibly, Axonn shrugged it off like it was a spring rain, saying only, "I renounce you."

The vortex was drawing close again. Axonn ignored it. Brutaka tore a hunk of stone from the wall and threw it, hitting Axonn dead-on. Axonn ignored that, too. "You don't exist, Brutaka. You are just a hollow shell without a spirit . . . a void."

Brutaka took a step backward. He had seen this happen once before. Axonn had been so consumed by a towering rage that nothing would bring him down. If the vortex did not claim him, he would crush Brutaka no matter what the cost in his own pain.

Axonn kept coming. Brutaka's eyes lit on the crystal vat. Zamor spheres filled with the virus in that vat had increased his strength in the past. Exposure to enough of it would make him vastly more powerful than Axonn. He took a few steps toward it.

The movement didn't escape Axonn. He stopped, reared back, and hurled his mighty axe.

Brutaka screamed in rage and frustration as he saw the weapon soar across the room and smash into the vat.

Razor-sharp shards of crystal flew everywhere. There was an explosion of darkness and sound as the virus was unleashed. The greenish-black cloud hovered for a moment near the ceiling before it began to dissipate, scattering to every corner of the fortress and beyond. Axonn could have sworn he heard a second scream then, one deeper and more guttural than Brutaka's. But he could see no source for such a sound.

Axonn's weapon was flying back toward him, but Brutaka knocked it to the ground with his sword. Then he advanced, slashing the air with his blade, determined to down his enemy. "Don't you realize you're fighting for a lost cause?" Brutaka snarled.

"Maybe," Axonn replied. "But don't you realize those are the only ones worth fighting for?"

Drawing on his last reserves of energy, Axonn unleashed a blast of pure power from his hands. It struck Brutaka like a tidal wave. For just a brief moment before he fell, the light of sanity seemed to return to Brutaka's eyes. Then those eyes closed and he hit the ground.

Axonn checked him to make sure he was still breathing. Then he picked up his axe and swung hard at the dimensional vortex. As Brutaka had predicted, his defeat had not caused the rift to disappear. The best Axonn could do was drive it away temporarily.

He turned around, planning to drag Brutaka out of the chamber before the vortex went after its creator. To his surprise, Botar was already there. Although he had seen this particular Order of Mata Nui member before, his appearance — lean, strong body topped by a monstrous head with a tooth-filled maw — never failed to startle him.

"Is this necessary?" Axonn asked.

"What is the law?" Botar replied.

"He made a mistake," said Axonn. "A bad one. But he doesn't deserve —"

Botar grabbed Brutaka and slung the

unconscious warrior over his shoulder. "He does. What is the law? The law is the will of Mata Nui. Break that law and only the pit will welcome you. Will you let him go . . . or will you challenge the law and risk sharing his fate, axe-wielder?"

Axonn's hand tightened on his weapon. He knew the miserable existence Brutaka now faced and it sickened him. But he also knew that in all of recorded history, no one had ever prevented Botar from doing his duty. Brutaka would be condemned to the pit, with or without Axonn's consent.

He followed Botar out of the chamber, stopping only for a glance at the dimensional vortex still swirling in the center of the room. Once outside the stronghold, Botar stopped.

"To darkness he turned, in darkness he will remain," Botar said.

"Not forever," Axonn replied. "Someday, I will find a way to free him."

Botar laughed. Coming from his fearsome jaws, it was a horrible sound. Then the Order of Mata Nui's gatherer of the fallen turned and walked away. Brutaka was on his way to the pit, the home of those so vile that the Order could do nothing but banish them from the light forever.

Axonn could do nothing but follow, the dimensional vortex Brutaka created forgotten. He was not inside the chamber to see two figures emerge from within the vortex. One was Toa-sized, her form shifting constantly as she adjusted to her new surroundings. The other was a huge Rahi, so gigantic he filled practically the entire chamber.

"Well, we're here," said the smaller of the two, "wherever 'here' might be. Somehow, I don't think we're in Metru Nui anymore, Tahtorak."

SEVEN

As they burst into the Chamber of Life, the Toa Inika were prepared for an ambush. They were even ready to wrest the Mask of Life away from the Piraka, if they had to. The one thing no one expected was to find four of the Piraka scattered like broken tools, while a rampaging brute and a Piraka atop a monstrous spider looked on. It was an image only a Brotherhood of Makuta member could love.

Vezon's eyes brightened when he saw the Toa. "How wonderful, more company!" he exclaimed. "The Piraka were amusing guests, but they break so easily. Are you made of sterner stuff? Of course you are. You're Toa, even with those very strange masks."

"Who are you? And how do you know who we are?" demanded Toa Jaller.

"I am Vezon, of course. And I know the

same way I know everything — the mask tells me," answered the bizarre figure. "Oh, not directly. But when I put it on, my eyes began to act strangely. You see?"

Twin shafts of red light shot from Vezon's eyes. In their gleam could be seen the six Toa Inika fighting for their lives against Fenrakk.

"Future sight," said Vezon. "I can see things — most things — before they happen. Not quite as much fun as making things explode with a glance, but hey, I take what I can get."

The brutish creature born from the two fused Piraka lumbered toward the Toa, ready for combat. Vezon sighed and fired a bolt of energy from his spear. It struck the creature, splitting it back into Vezok and Reidak. The two Piraka, shocked by the sudden separation, collapsed.

"They call it the Mask of Life," Vezon said. "But it might as well be a Mask of Death. Ask anyone who has tried to get their hands on it. And in a few moments we'll have six more for the lava, won't we, Fenrakk?"

Vezon's monstrous pet advanced on the

Toa. Hewkii snapped off a stalactite and hurled it, blunt end first, at the wall. It ricocheted twice before heading right for the mask. Vezon spotted it out of the corner of his eye at the last second and shifted so that the projectile struck his shoulder. Amazingly, it did not seem to do anything more than annoy him.

"Like to throw things, hmmm?" he said softly. He yanked on the chain and Fenrakk slammed its foreleg onto the ground, sending huge chunks of stone flying straight up in the air. Vezon caught one three feet in diameter and flung it at Hewkii. The Toa ducked as the rock slammed into the wall. A large fragment struck him in the chest and knocked the breath from his lungs.

The other Toa snapped into action. Nuparu and Matoro hurled earth and ice at Vezon, but neither seemed to faze him. Jaller used his flame power to bring down part of the stone ceiling, only to see Vezon bat it away. Then Hahli and Kongu took up the attack, faring no better than their partners. If anything, Vezon and Fenrakk seemed to be getting stronger.

"All done?" asked Vezon. "It's my turn."

Fenrakk charged at impossible speed. Vezon caught Jaller with the flat of his spear and hurled the Toa of Fire across the chamber. Nuparu rocketed into the air in time to catch his team leader before Jaller was smashed against the rock. Down below, Hewkii tried to come at Fenrakk from behind, only to be flattened by a blow from one of the spider's legs.

The battle became a nightmarish blur. Vezon and Fenrakk were everywhere at once, battering the Toa into the ground. The more the Toa fought back, the harder they were struck down. When it looked as if he had easily won, Vezon reined Fenrakk to a halt.

"Poor Toa," he said. "Relying so much on your strength and your weapons and your elemental powers, and not a one of them will do you any good here. Watch."

Vezon picked up a rock and struck Fenrakk

with it as hard as he could. He did it again, and yet a third time. The Rahi never stirred, but the Toa could have sworn the beast actually looked more powerful.

"The power of motion," Vezon said, smiling. "Any blow is only as strong as the motion that delivers it, and I feed on the energy that fuels that motion. When you strike me, when I strike you, I get stronger. Oh, and I shared my power with Fenrakk here, of course — it's only polite."

Jaller, his body aching, forced himself to stand. "We ... didn't come all this way ... only to lose."

Vezon smiled. "Don't be silly. Of course you did. Do you know how many have tried to get their hands on this mask over the millennia? And do you know what happened to them? I'll give you a hint: the lucky ones only went mad."

"If the mask is so terribly dangerous, why did the Piraka want it so badly?" asked Hahli.

"Because they're fools!" snapped Vezon. Fenrakk hissed and spat acidic saliva on the stone floor.

"Yet they thought they could get it," said Matoro. "Or . . . someone thought they could."

Vezon beamed. "Smart, smart, smart. Isn't he just as bright as a new Kanohi mask, Fenrakk? It will almost be a shame to shatter him into ice crystals, won't it?"

Nuparu staggered to his feet. In the midst of trying to make the room stop spinning, he had caught Matoro's remark. "So somebody put them up to this? Who? Why?"

"No way to guess the who," said Jaller. "But the why? You risk death a hundred times trying to make it to the Mask of Life, and evidently you risk worse by actually getting it. The Piraka were expendable. If they died trying to carry out their mission, it would be no great loss, and whoever gave them the idea to do this could just try again."

"Not if we get the mask," said Hewkii, now fully recovered. "So let's swat the spider and take it!"

"Haven't you learned you can't defeat me?" said Vezon. "All you can do is amuse me."

"Then loud-laugh this off, you lunatic," said Kongu. Summoning his power of air, he created a cyclone centered on Vezon and Fenrakk. Whirling at incredible speed, it sucked the air out of their lungs. The Toa of Air couldn't maintain it for long, but by the time he stopped, the pair were obviously weakened.

"Your turn, Hahli," said Kongu.

The Toa Inika of Water called on her power to draw the moisture out of the air around her foes, dehydrating them. At the same time, Matoro made the temperature immediately around Vezon plunge far below zero in a fraction of a second.

"Give it up, Vezon," said Jaller. "We don't have to hit you to hurt you."

Vezon didn't answer, simply shook his head. Fenrakk was pounding its right foreleg on the stone floor, slowly, over and over again. It would have seemed a harmless gesture, if the Toa didn't know what they knew.

The impact, Jaller realized. *Fenrakk is using*

the energy behind its blows to the floor to restore its strength!

The knowledge came too late. Fenrakk was already back to full power, charging ahead at the behest of its mad rider. Hahli and Matoro were struck head-on and flung against the walls. Fenrakk went for Kongu next, but Nuparu flew in and grabbed the Toa of Air before the spider's blow could land.

There was no more time to waste. Toa Jaller took aim with his energized flame sword. "Go ahead!" shouted Vezon. "Sizzle me, shock me — you'll only make me stronger!"

"Who said I was aiming at you?" Jaller replied, unleashing a blast of flame and lightning. It struck the floor beneath Fenrakk, turning the stone to molten rock. Startled, the massive spider retreated. Suddenly one of its back legs slipped on the ledge of the lava channel. The creature lost its balance.

What followed next was one of the strangest sights the Toa had ever seen. Unable to jump off the Rahi, Vezon seemed instead to be urging it into the lava. Rahi and rider toppled over, vanishing beneath the fiery crimson river without even a scream.

"Mata Nui preserve us," Nuparu said, shocked. "He . . . he did that to himself!"

"And took the Mask of Life with him," added Toa Jaller. "I have to go in there after it."

"Jaller, no!" said Hewkii. "You won't last more than ten seconds in that cauldron!"

"That's ten seconds longer than any of the rest of you would," the Toa leader answered. "With my natural resistance to heat and flame, maybe I can buy enough time to retrieve the mask and toss it to you. After that . . . take over as leader, Hewkii. Keep the team together and get the Mask of Life wherever it has to go."

Jaller turned away and walked to the edge of the lava river. He could feel the intense heat coming up at him in waves. As an experienced lava surfer, he was more than familiar with the sight, the smell, even the sound of molten rock as it flowed — and he also knew all too well what it could do to someone unlucky enough to be exposed to it. He had once seen an injured Kane-Ra bull stumble into a lava pit in Ta-Wahi. It was a sight he would never forget.

If he waited any longer, the others might talk him out of doing what he knew he had to do. He braced himself and prepared to leap. Suddenly something broke the surface of the lava. Jaller couldn't believe his eyes — it was the Mask of Life! It had floated to the surface, intact! It was close enough to touch! It was . . . still grafted to a very much alive Vezon.

Jaller stumbled backward in surprise. Vezon was rising out of the lava, looking as if he had just taken a refreshing swim. But the creature he was riding was not Fenrakk. No, the spider Rahi was gone — the even more massive beast emerging from the lava looked like a huge serpent. It casually swiped at Jaller with one of its claws. The force of even this glancing blow sent the Toa flying into Hewkii and almost knocked him unconscious.

"Why so startled?" Vezon asked, glancing

at each Toa Inika in turn. "Did you think that I had left you for good?"

The Rahi dragon opened its mouth and exhaled a powerful blast of energy, sufficient to flatten all six Toa. Then it took two great strides forward and looked around, evidently surprised that its small foes were still breathing.

"Who is this, you wonder?" Vezon continued. "Where is Fenrakk? Well, my friends, this *is* Fenrakk . . . in a way. It is all part of the mask's curse. Defeat us however many times you like, we will always come back more powerful than before. Should you drive my new friend here — who I have named Kardas, by the way — down to certain destruction, it will simply rise again, in some worse form. And I will be right there with it."

Kongu took advantage of Vezon's boasting to aim and fire an energy bolt. The shaft stung Kardas, who evidently did not share Fenrakk's ability to absorb the force of the blow. The Rahi responded with a blast of its own, which drove Kongu over the lava channel and into a stone wall. The rock shattered at the impact of his body and the Toa of Air found himself falling through into another chamber.

"Good Kardas," Vezon cooed, patting his mount on the back of the neck. "Nice devastating monster. Are you my favorite engine of destruction? Yes, you are." He looked back at the shaken Toa. "Energy — Kardas produces it nonstop. So it's either release it by blasting you, or else go boom himself. Which did you think we would choose?"

Hahli fired her energy harpoon paired with a powerful blast of water laced with lightning. "And you're known for your good choices, aren't you? That's how you wound up a master of monsters!"

Both of her attacks struck home. Kardas responded with another blast, but Hahli dove beneath it. The energy blew apart a section of the wall behind her.

"Now see what you're making him do?" Vezon scolded. "I have to live here, you know!"

Kardas charged. Matoro responded by

freezing the stone beneath the monster's feet. As it began to slide, Hewkii triggered his elemental power and made a powerful fist of rock erupt from beneath the ice. It slammed into Kardas, sending beast and Vezon stumbling backward.

"Nice to have something to hit again," Hewkii said, smiling.

Nuparu took flight, peppering the ground around Kardas with energy bolts from his laser drill. Kardas blasted back, striking Nuparu as he tried to dodge in midair. He plummeted like a rock, only to be caught by Hewkii.

"We have to all strike at once," said the Toa Inika of Stone. He gathered Hahli and Matoro, but Jaller and Kongu were still out of the fight. The four Toa hurled their elemental powers at Kardas simultaneously. The beast roared and let loose a blast of energy which struck theirs head-on. The two surges of power battled each other for supremacy in the middle of the chamber. At first, the Toa seemed to be winning. But their enemy's reserves were inexhaustible. Little by little, Kardas' explosive power overwhelmed them.

"Get down!" Hewkii shouted, but it was too late. The energy hit them like a pile driver and they fell, battered and dazed.

Vezon smiled. "That's better. Now I wonder what the Spear of Fusion could do with the four of you? Or maybe I should use it on each of you alone, and see if I can split the Matoran you used to be from the arrogant fools you are now?"

Toa Jaller revived in time to hear this and see the danger his friends were in. He glanced to the side and saw Kongu crawling back through the hole in the wall. "I have an idea," he whispered.

"Good," Kongu replied. "Hope it starts with, 'Mata Nui is just taking it easy for a while and he'll feel better. Let's go home.'"

"I need you to use your mask in a way you haven't before," Jaller said. "I'm not sure, but I think there's more to the Mask of Life than we know. Remember what Umbra said? It created the protodax to guard it. Kongu, it may be that mask is capable of some kind of thought!"

"So it's evidently one up on you," Kongu said. "Masks don't think."

"This one does," Jaller insisted. "Maybe not like we do, but . . . Use your Mask of Telepathy. Try to read the mask's thoughts and then project them into Vezon's mind. If you can distract him for a few moments, I think I know how to end this."

Any idea Toa Kongu had about arguing further was banished by the sight of Vezon aiming his spear at Hahli, Hewkii, Matoro, and Nuparu. Still doubting this idea had any chance of working, he focused the power of his mask on the Mask of Life fused to Vezon. At first, all he "heard" was silence. Then there was a jumble of colors and images and sounds all running together like a fast-moving stream. He almost broke off the contact then, as much out of shock as the difficulty of interpreting what he was encountering.

Kongu took a deep breath and kept on. Now the images were beginning to take on clearer shape. He saw Vezon and Kardas . . . he saw Matoro . . . the Mask of Life knew the sacrifice Matoro had been willing to make. It knew that Matoro had long borne the burden of secret knowledge, things he had learned from the

Turaga but had been forbidden to share with other Matoran.

The mask knew one thing more as well, something even Kongu had not known. On the journey to Voya Nui, Matoro and the others had traveled through a pitch-dark tunnel. Along the way, Matoro had stumbled over what felt like a living being and had reached out a hand to help. A hand clasped his and Matoro had led what he thought was one of his friends out of the tunnel and into the light. When he made it out the other end, however, he saw that Jaller, Hewkii, and all the rest were already there. Turning around, he saw that no one was holding his hand, even though he still could feel that cold grip. Startled and frightened, he had never told anyone about this.

Now Kongu could see what had truly happened. The power of the Mask of Life was so great that it had reached out to Matoro even over so vast a distance. Even wandering in darkness, Matoro had shown a willingness to help someone he perceived to be in need — never realizing that "someone" was just a manifestation of the mask's power.

Abruptly, the mask's feelings became crystal clear. It despised Vezon, thought of the Piraka as less than nothing, barely worthy of the life that infused him. If it were possible, it would have withdrawn its curse and let Vezon take his chances in battle. What it truly wanted was a new guardian: Matoro.

Kongu gasped at that revelation. Then he realized there would be time to be shocked later. He had a job to do. Fighting the strain, he grasped the mask's thoughts and forced them into Vezon's mind.

The effect was immediate. Vezon and Kardas stopped dead. Rage and grief warred on Vezon's face as he realized he had been condemned for eternity to serve a mask that held him in contempt. The object he fought so hard to protect wanted to abandon him like he was trash. It was more than Vezon's already unstable mind could accept.

"No!" he shouted, his voice ragged. "I did

everything you asked! I beat the Piraka! I beat the Toa! No one is touching you, no one is taking you from this place, ever! And I won't be gotten rid of after all this — I won't!"

Vezon's crimson eyes fixed on Matoro. "So it wants you, does it?" he hissed, aiming his spear at the dazed Toa Inika of Ice. "Let's see if it still does when I'm through with you. You can be the ultimate chamber guard, Toa, once you are fused forever with the lava that courses through this chamber."

Jaller saw the energies begin to crackle around the head of the spear. Moving faster than he ever had, he loaded the special zamor sphere Axonn had given him. Axonn had said the Toa would need it if they ever hoped to retrieve the Mask of Life. Jaller hoped he was right and that now was the time to use it.

He fired his launcher. The zamor sphere struck Vezon. Instantly, a shimmering glow enveloped both the Piraka and Kardas, freezing them both in mid-motion. Jaller didn't take time to analyze what had just happened. He motioned to

Kongu and they ran to their friends, helping the four Toa to their feet and making sure they were all right.

"I'm okay," said Hahli. "What did you do to them? Are they . . . dead?"

"No," said Jaller. Then seeing the madness and loss reflected on Vezon's features, he added, "Something much worse — they're still alive."

"We have to get the mask now, while we can," said Hewkii, starting for Vezon.

"Let Matoro do it," Kongu said.

The other Toa looked at him, puzzled. "Why?" said Hewkii. "What difference does it make who —?"

"Just . . . just let Matoro do it, okay?"

Hewkii shrugged. Matoro circled behind the frozen figures and reached into the field of energy. Grasping the Mask of Life with both hands, he was ready to pull with all his strength to wrench it free. To his surprise, it came off easily. Although it was a standard Kanohi mask made of metallic protodermis, it felt warm to the touch, almost as if it really was alive.

"I've got it! I've got it!" he shouted.

"Excellent. And we have you."

The Toa Inika spun around. Zaktan and the other five Piraka were standing there, ready for battle. "You have defeated Vezon and his monster," the Piraka leader said. "In gratitude, we will destroy you as quickly and efficiently as possible and take the mask. No need to thank us — that is just the type of beings we are."

EIGHT

The Matoran resistance members led the Toa Nuva up to the main floor of the Piraka stronghold. The building was in sad shape, with entire walls blown out by the battles that had been fought there. Now all was quiet. The Matoran almost dreaded what they might see — what if the Inika had lost? To their surprise, there were no bodies to be seen.

The virus chamber had changed significantly. The crystal vat had been shattered and there was no sign of the antidermis virus anywhere. Another wall had been smashed, evidently by a being or force more powerful than any yet unleashed in the room. Even the rubble had been pulverized.

"What went through there?" wondered Kazi.

"One problem at a time," answered Balta. "The Kanohi masks are through here."

The Matoran watched in silence as the Toa Nuva reclaimed their masks. The act seemed to re-energize them. Tahu Nuva turned to Garan and shook the Onu-Matoran's hand.

"We thank you," he said. "Now where are these Toa Inika you spoke of?"

"I wish I knew," Garan replied. "Toa Jaller said —"

"Wait a moment," Tahu interrupted. "*Toa* Jaller?"

"That's right, he and Toa Kongu and Toa Matoro —"

Lewa Nuva chuckled. "Kongu a Toa-hero? Oh, this I must see."

"When you are finished being amused, Lewa, they may well need our help," said Kopaka.

Garan nodded. "Here's hoping they aren't already beyond help."

Zaktan smiled. "We have been awake for some time now, of course. We just felt it made more sense for you to exhaust yourselves in battle for the Mask of Life. Now that you have it, we will take it."

"You mean you'll try," said Hewkii. "And fail."

Both sides braced for the fight, but it was not to happen. The effect of the zamor sphere on Vezon and Kardas had faded. Although it left both too weak to be a threat for the moment, Kardas was not going to be defeated so easily. As the beast collapsed, it unleashed one last blast of energy that struck Matoro. The shock made him lose his grip on the Mask of Life.

The Piraka started forward, ready to scramble for the mask when it hit the ground — except it never did fall to the floor. Instead, it hovered in midair before flashing out of the chamber almost too fast for the eye to follow. It was headed back the way the Toa and Piraka had come.

Zaktan and his team turned to go after it. The Toa Inika ran forward, too, determined to get it first. "Hewkii!" Jaller shouted, pointing at the Piraka.

The Toa Inika of Stone nodded and loosed

his elemental powers on the enemy. Stone vises erupted from the floor to grab all six Piraka and hold them fast. Zaktan avoided the trap by dissipating into a swarm of protodites, only to be flash-frozen in the next moment by Matoro.

"That buys us maybe ten seconds," said Hewkii.

"Then that will have to be enough," Jaller replied, racing up the staircase.

The six Toa Inika ran as if their very universe depended on it, for in truth it did. So fast were they moving that they did not notice the words of fire forming on the stairs beneath their feet . . . words that read:

Beware the depths of darkness
That wait with chill embrace,
For those doomed to dwell within the pit
Can never leave that place.

No one will know your fate
If taken by the shadowed sea,
Only whispers of the waves will say

Death has at last claimed thee.

As Hewkii had predicted, it took the Piraka only seconds to shatter their bonds. They debated for a moment whether to free Zaktan or not, then decided they would need their full strength to stop the Toa Inika.

"What about Vezon?" said Thok. "He's still alive. Do we just leave him here?"

"No," snarled Vezok. "We don't." He marched toward the Spear of Fusion, saying, "Someone use this on me and Vezon. I want to be one being again."

"We don't have time for that!" snapped Zaktan. "Come on!"

"No!" yelled Vezok. "We do this now!"

Zaktan nodded at Reidak. The ebon-armored Piraka reached Vezok in two quick strides and brushed him aside. Then he seized the Spear of Fusion and, before Vezok could react, broke it in two, and then broke both halves again. Satisfied, he threw the pieces at Vezok's feet.

"There. Done. Let's go," said Reidak. "Or do you want some of the same?"

The Toa Inika had been lucky. Their passage back up the staircase had been unimpeded by guardians. Apparently, the mask's protectors were in place to stop anyone from reaching the lower chamber, not those fleeing from it.

Still, the mask managed to stay just ahead of them. Attempts to use elemental powers to slow it down or stop it all met with failure. Matoro offered to unleash his spirit and have it fly ahead to see where the mask was heading, but Jaller turned him down. He wasn't going to leave Matoro's body unprotected on this staircase with the Piraka right behind.

The Mask of Life shot out of the stairway entrance and into a driving rainstorm. The Toa followed right after it, fighting to keep pace. The many rounds of battle, followed by this chase, had made their limbs feel like lead and their lungs burn with exhaustion.

The mask never hesitated. It shot away to

the north, heading for the bay. Nuparu launched himself into the sky and flew after it, at one time almost coming close enough to grab it. It seemed like every time the mask was lost from view of the other Toa Inika, it would slow down slightly, as if it wanted them to keep up.

"It's leading us somewhere," Nuparu shouted down. "I don't see any traps ahead, though."

"If you could easy-see them," grumbled Kongu, "then they wouldn't be very good traps."

The chase continued over rocky slopes until both mask and Toa reached the icy coast-line. The mask flew past the edge of the land and hovered for just a moment before plunging into the water. Toa Hahli immediately went after it. As soon as she dove, Matoro's body collapsed as his spirit went to follow her down.

The Mask of Life was easy to follow even in the murky water, for it gave off a telltale glow. Not so easy was going down after it, as the pressure increased beyond even the toler-ance of a Toa of Water. More than once, Hahli wished she had Toa Nuva Gali's Mask of Water

Breathing to sustain her. Her lungs were desperate for air and the mask was no closer to being in her grasp.

Suddenly, she faltered. The water pressure increased abruptly, forcing air from her lungs. Water rushed in to fill the void and Hahli began to drown. Matoro watched in horror, unable to affect her physically while in spirit form. His only hope was to flash back to the surface and get the others.

He was gone in an instant. He never saw the small shape swimming rapidly up from the depths toward Hahli.

Back on the coastline, Matoro's body suddenly bolted up from the ground. "Hahli's drowning!"

The other Toa made for the water, Jaller already figuring out a rescue plan. He never had to use it. Hahli's body suddenly appeared on the surface. All five Inika wondered if they had been too late, and their companion was dead.

Then she sputtered and coughed, the sweetest sound any of the Inika had ever heard. Jaller went to pull her back to shore. That was when he noticed someone was already holding her.

A head broke the surface, wearing a Kanohi mask. It was a Matoran! Toa Jaller helped both him and Hahli to the beach. The Toa of Water was already recovering, but the Matoran collapsed as soon as he hit land.

"Who are you?" said Jaller. "Where did you come from?"

"No time," gasped the Matoran. "Help us . . . city beneath the sea . . . help us or we're lost. . . ."

"What city?" asked Hewkii. "What are you talking about?"

But the Matoran wasn't saying any more. His heartlight stopped shining and his eyes faded to black. He was dead.

The Piraka had seen the entire turn of events from up among the rocks. The Mask of Life was lost, temporarily, and the Toa Inika were exhausted and confused. It was a perfect time to strike.

"We'll split up," said Zaktan. "I'll take Reidak

and Vezok this way. Hakann, Thok, and Avak, attack from the left. We'll trap them between us."

The two teams started in opposite directions, but had gone only a little way when Avak said, "Wait! Look!"

On the edge of the jungle, the Piraka could see a most unwelcome assemblage of beings. The six Matoran who had made up the Voya Nui resistance were standing with Axonn and the freed Toa Nuva. A defeated Brutaka was being carried by some entity the Piraka did not know, and that same being was deep in conversation with Tahu Nuva. As they watched, the strange being and Brutaka vanished in a wisp of smoke.

"Does anyone think we can beat twelve Toa and Axonn, without Brutaka's help?" asked Thok. When no one answered, he added, "Didn't think so."

"So that's it? We give up?" said Reidak.

Zaktan's protodites buzzed angrily. "No. We've come too far for that."

"Not to mention that having the Mask of Life is the only thing that will keep us safe from the Dark Hunters when we leave this island," said Hakann. "I doubt the Shadowed One was very pleased with our defection."

"We watch," said Zaktan. "And we wait for the perfect time to strike. Let the Toa think we are defeated and have fled Voya Nui. That is the Toa's greatest weakness — they are always so quick to believe they have won."

Matoro stood over the body of the dead villager. "Mata Nui watch over him."

"He sacrificed his life to save mine," said Toa Hahli. "That may make him a greater hero than any of us."

"And he brought us more mysteries," said Hewkii. "Who was this Matoran? What killed him? What city was he talking about? And why did the Mask of Life vanish beneath the waves?"

Toa Kongu shook his head. "Why do I deep-think we're all about to go for a swim?"

Epilogue

The six Toa Inika stood on the beach, gazing at the dark water and lost in their own thoughts. Some, like Jaller, pondered the fate of the Mask of Life. Others wondered if the Matoran was telling the truth and there really was a Matoran city beneath the sea. Regardless, the missing mask and deceased Matoran added up to the same thing in their minds.

"Maybe fate random-picked the wrong Matoran to be Toa," said Kongu. "We failed."

"No, Toa-hero, you succeeded," a familiar voice said. "Now you just have to succeed again."

Kongu and the other Toa Inika whirled in surprise. Coming down the beach, led by Axonn and the six members of the Matoran resistance, were the Toa Nuva. All of them had their Kanohi Nuva masks and their equipment and looked none the worse for their experiences on the island.

"Tahu!" Jaller shouted. "Gali! I can't believe it!"

"We were afraid you might be dead!" said Hahli. "It's so wonderful to see you. Now everything will be all right."

"Toa are hard to kill, you know that," said Pohatu Nuva, smiling. "Ask Makuta . . . if he ever gets out from under that door."

"Our Matoran friends found us," said Tahu Nuva, "and freed us from the effects of the Piraka's zamor spheres. One even offered to forge a new air katana for Lewa. By the way, where are the Piraka?"

Jaller swiftly related the events leading up to the discovery and loss of the Mask of Life. Tahu listened intently, and reacted with surprise to the news that a Matoran civilization might lie hidden under the sea.

"We were trying to come up with a way to follow the mask when you arrived," said Jaller. "But now that you're here, you can go with us."

"Or maybe you would rather we just went back to Metru Nui?" asked Nuparu. Secretly, he hoped the Toa Nuva would brush aside that question. Having tasted the adventure of being a Toa, he had no wish to go back to guard duty on Metru Nui.

The six Toa Nuva glanced at each other. Kopaka nodded. Gali put a reassuring hand on Tahu's shoulder. Then the Toa Nuva of Fire turned back to the Toa Inika. "I think, perhaps, it is we who should return to the city," Tahu said. "Take your team, Jaller, and find the mask."

"What?" Jaller said, stunned. "But you are Toa Nuva — the most powerful of all Toa — and this is your destiny!"

"It is our destiny to awaken Mata Nui from his centuries-long slumber," Kopaka corrected. "You are fighting to save the life of the Great Spirit, which must be done before he can be returned to consciousness. And that, my friends, is your destiny — not ours."

"We came to Voya Nui to find the Mask of Life," said Gali Nuva. "We failed. If it were not for you six, we and the Matoran of this island would still be enslaved to the Piraka . . . or worse. Don't you see? Your very existence as Toa is a sign from the Great Beings that you were meant to find the mask and save Mata Nui."

Jaller didn't want to accept it, but he knew there was truth in Gali's words. Where the Toa Nuva had met defeat, his team of Toa Inika had succeeded, at least temporarily. That had to mean something, unless the universe was just playing a cruel joke.

"What about the Matoran here?" asked Hahli. "The Piraka are still on the loose. The villagers are still in danger."

Tahu Nuva hesitated before replying. He hadn't thought of that. Back on Metru Nui, the Matoran had the Toa of Light and the Turaga to look after them while the Toa Nuva were away. Here there were no Turaga or Toa to serve as protectors. Should they take the Matoran back with them to Metru Nui?

Before a decision could be reached, Axonn

spoke up. "There is no need to be concerned," he said. "I will remain on Voya Nui and see to the Matoran. We will rebuild their lives here, until destiny says it is time for them to leave."

Jaller didn't know what to say. Axonn had been a mighty ally, and the Toa Nuva far more than that. How could he and his friends say good-bye? And with the mask out of reach under the ocean, was there even a point to a farewell?

As if anticipating his worries, Axonn spoke again. "Fear not, my friend. There is a way to reach the undersea realm, but the way is treacherous . . . and your destination a place of death and despair. But if you are willing to make the journey, my axe can open the way for you."

This time, Jaller did not look to his partners for their consent. He already knew what their answer would be. "We'll do it," he said.

"Then meet me at the Matoran village in the center of the island," said Axonn. "Your quest begins there."

The good-byes between the Toa Inika and

the Toa Nuva were short and simple. Hands were clasped, words of encouragement exchanged, and assurances were given that this was not the last time they would see each other. When the time came to part, Tahu Nuva said, "Go now, Toa Inika. As Matoran, you showed courage and heart as great as that of any Toa. As heroes, you have proven yourselves worthy of joining the ranks of the greatest in legend. We will be waiting to greet you when you have fulfilled your destiny."

Axonn stood beside Tahu Nuva as the Toa Inika walked away. When the six new heroes were lost from sight, the mighty guardian turned to Tahu and said, "They are gone. But I do not need to be wearing the Mask of Truth to know you lied to them."

Tahu kept staring straight ahead. "Where we have to go, they can't follow. What we have to do, they cannot be part of. And you know it."

Axonn nodded. "Do you think the Toa Inika will succeed?"

Tahu Nuva turned away. "I think they can count themselves very lucky if they survive."

* * *

A short time later, Axonn joined the Toa Inika in the center of the Matoran village. "This is the beginning," the guardian said. "And Mata Nui will help see you through to the end."

He unlimbered his axe and swung it at the ground once, twice, thrice, four times. His blows tore through soil and rock until he had dug a great pit. The floor of the pit was strange white stone. Axonn raised his weapon once more and threw it into the hole, smashing the white stone to bits and revealing a passage beyond.

"Your route lies through there," Axonn said as his axe returned to his hand. "It will take you to the city beneath the sea and the Mask of Life . . . but take care, Toa. The ocean is home to many wonders, and many dangers . . . to figures of great courage, and some so evil that even the Order of Mata Nui could do nothing but banish them below."

One by one, the Toa Inika climbed down

into the pit and vanished into the darkness. Axonn watched them go, not sure what he felt more — fear for the Toa, about to face horrors beyond imagining . . . or fear for the fate of the universe, if they should fail in their quest.